The Wizard

By

Randy Corn

Forward

For ten thousand years the seven wizards of the Wizard Council of Eonor had governed and protected the Elven folk of Eonor. As their time was passing and no apprentice was born to pass on their knowledge, the council put all their knowledge and magic into the "White Book of Magic". It was established that only a true wizard could read from the book. A true wizard was defined as one who is born when a comet is visible during a total eclipse and can read from the book.

Gindon, a member of the council could not accept his demise. He sought to increase his power and extend his life. He wrote the "Black Book of Magic" which, advised him to kill the other wizards and take their power as the only solution to becoming immortal. He killed one of the wizards and with a terrible war looming, the Elven folk and the youngest of the Wizard Council left for a new land to call home or "Urot".

Gindon was able to kill another wizard and became more powerful. He gave the "Black Book of Magic" to his daughter, Gelda, and sent her with the others, to the new land.

Massive fires and explosions were seen as the ship sailed off to their new home. Gelda knew her father had been killed and sought revenge against the Elven folk.

The ships landed on the shore of Urot, the sight of their first city, Windor.

Gelda, seeking revenge for her father's death, conjured a troll that killed several Elves before being slain. Gelda was accused of practicing Black Magic and was banished to the Black Mountains since Elven do not kill Elven. She swore her revenge and cursed them as she left.

Gelda learned the ways of Black Magic and conjured more slave creatures to build her fortress castle.

As the Elven folk expanded their realm, they discovered humans living in the prairies, forests, and mountains. They were primitive but saw that they were intelligent and gentle. They taught humans woodworking, metallurgy, reading, and writing. After a time, humans built their own cities and villages. They kept good relations with the Elven folk, and it was not uncommon for humans and Elves to marry.

And so, it was with King Roland Drakorne who married the Elven Princess Errisa and soon their son Ferryman was born when a comet was visible during a total eclipse.

The people of Urot wait patiently for a wizard's apprentice to be declared as Gelda plots their demise.

Chapter 1

The Rise of the Troll King

Thirteen-year-old Ferryman Drakorne stood at the podium. The White Book of Magic lay on a pedestal in front of him. A large crowd of Elven and men folk stood before him, waiting in anticipation to see if he could read the book. He was their last hope for a wizard's apprentice.

Ferryman's father, King Roland, had invited all the royal families of the realm to attend the Wizard's Festival. Many generations had come and gone since the Elven folk landed on the shores of Urot. The wizard Pantul had long since reached the twilight of his life and the folks of the realm feared that he would pass before an apprentice would be born. Ferryman, along with several other children had been born thirteen years earlier when a comet was visible during a total eclipse, a sign that signaled the birth of a wizard as prophesized long ago by the Wizard Council of Eonor.

Ferryman saw Keira in the crowd. He couldn't help but stare at her. She stared back at him with her bright blue eyes. His mind drifted into a dream state as his heartbeat raced, and a warm feeling came over him.

"Uh-Um! Ferryman." Pantul cleared his throat.

Ferryman looked back at Pantul, then he looked back at the crowd. Ferryman was nervous and sweat tickled his forehead. When he opened the book, the crowd grew very quiet.

"By prophecy of the Wizard Council of Eonor, only a true wizard may read the words of the White Book of Magic. I, your name, I mean, Ferryman Drakorne, have been chosen as the wizard's apprentice," Ferryman read.

Ferryman's feat left everyone speechless except Keira.

"Hail Ferryman the wizard's apprentice," shouted Keira.

"Hail Ferryman," roared the crowd.

King Roland stood up. Others congratulated him. The king raised his mug of ale. "To my son. The wizard's apprentice!"

Everyone raised their mugs.

"To Ferryman. The wizard's apprentice," the crowd roared.

Ferryman felt a chill of fear run up and down his spine. Being a wizard was a great responsibility and he wasn't sure if he was up to the task. He turned to Pantul. "Are you sure there hasn't been a mistake?"

Pantul kneeled down and put his hand on Ferryman's shoulder. "The White Book of Magic does not make mistakes. It only chooses those who are true wizards."

"If I'm the first to be chosen, then how do you know it isn't making a mistake?" Ferryman shuffled his feet.

Pantul looked at him rather curiously. "You think like a wizard. Trust the book, young Ferryman. It will never steer you wrong."

Ferryman looked at the faces in the crowd that was still shouting his name. He felt like running away and hiding but then he saw her again; her smile with bright blue eyes and long brown hair. At that moment nothing else mattered but the warm feeling in his heart.

Ferryman forged his way through the crowd to get to her. He had to know who she was and nothing was going to stop him.

The night sky was clear and the moon was full. The minstrels played Elven music as the folks danced merrily around a roasting spit where an Eglort, a giant flightless bird of prey, was being roasted. It was so large it took three big strong villagers to turn the giant beast over the spit and another to baste it. Sparks from the fire were caught by the warm summer breeze and hurled up into the night sky. Many folks danced while others drank their ale and watched.

The kings and queens of the realm were seated with King Roland Drakorne, the king of men, and his Elven wife Queen Errisa, who ruled over the village of Beldredor. The wizard Pantul Ryme sat with them anticipating a demonstration of his wizardry.

As the folks danced in merriment, four big strong villagers made their way through the dense crowd. Everyone moved aside to allow them to pass as they carried a most cherished delight, a giant vanilla frosted cherry nut cake, the likes of which no Elven or man-folk could resist. It was Queen Errisa's family recipe, baked to pure perfection and giving off an aroma that made mouths water. Children eagerly followed behind the men carrying the treat.

After a time Pantul stood up with his long white beard and hair blowing in the light summer breeze and his wizard's staff firmly grasped in his right hand. Pantul raised his staff high above his head and uttered loudly the incantation, "Illumina numinor hipiddi hopper."

A fireball shot from the end of the staff and streaked upward through the night sky as everyone stopped and stared in wonder.

The fireball exploded, forming a giant illuminated rabbit that hopped across the sky and dissolved into a swirling mass of colored lights.

Everyone cheered as Pantul proudly took his bows.

*

Gelda, the Elven witch of the Black Mountains, was in her castle laboratory with her beastly servant. She had the look of a young woman in her early thirties even though she was nearly three hundred years old. She stood in her purple hooded robe reading a passage from the Black Book of Magic as she rubbed a black seeing orb.

"Uta basnoctu trotchni wizdrin visomtu," she cried out.

The image of the wizard's festival appeared in the seeing orb. She turned toward her beastly servant, smiling as it cowered before her. She turned her attention back to the orb.

"Look at them. The fools. They don't suspect a thing." Gelda laughed hideously. "Uta basnoctu Beloche."

An image of Beloche, the Troll King appeared in the orb. He and his army of trolls waited in the Ont Forest just beyond the plain, a few miles from Beldredor.

Beloche, the Troll King, and his army of trolls waited for instructions. The Troll King was very large and was greatly feared by the other trolls, for he wielded a scepter of great power. He gazed into a seeing orb, which another troll was carrying. Gelda's image appeared in the orb.

"Burn the village to the ground! Kill them! Bring that fool Pantul and the boy apprentice to me. Alive! Their power will restore my beauty. Fail me and I will feed you to the wolves," shouted Gelda.

The Troll King grinned at her, with his lower fangs protruding from his mouth. He grunted assent.

All the trolls begin to wail.

Dingle and Bailey were the guards manning the village tower as they watched the festivities in the square. Bailey looked out over the plain. He heard a faint sound in the distance. "Did you hear something?".

"Like what?" Dingle didn't take his eyes off the dancing below.

"I don't know. I've never heard it before." Bailey's stomach growled.

"It must have been your stomach you heard," said Dingle laughing.

Ferryman stood before Keira. She was wearing a wreath of white flowers on top of her head. Her pointed ears protruded through her long flowing hair. Ferryman was so nervous his mind went blank.

"Hi. I'm Ferryman," he said after getting up his nerve.

"I know. I mean it's nice to meet you. I'm Keira." She smiled.

They both giggled.

"Young Ferryman. Come here. It's time for you to cut the cake," yelled the Elven baker.

Ferryman grabbed hold of Keira's hand and led her over to the cake. The Elven baker handed Ferryman a dagger to cut the cake with. Ferryman did the honors and gave Keira the first piece.

The moon passed behind a large cloud. The Troll King raised his scepter and then pointed it toward the village. The other trolls took notice immediately.

The Troll King bellowed out a command.

The troll army made hideous noises as they emerged from the forest wearing armor and wielding various weapons. They ran faster and faster toward the village.

In the tower, Bailey looked out over the plain, as the strange sounds grew louder. He became apprehensive as the tower vibrated.

Keira and Ferryman went off together to eat their cake. She pointed to a stocky man with a weathered face. "That's my father over there. He's a farmer," she said happily.

"I've had your father's tomatoes. They're the best I've ever eaten." Ferryman smiled.

She smiled back. Ferryman pointed to her nose, which had a spot of icing on it. They giggled as he wiped it off.

The guards felt the tower vibrating more vigorously. Bailey looked out over the dark plain and heard a sound akin to thunder. They could see nothing until the moon peered out from behind the clouds revealing the Troll

King and his army barreling toward the village at an alarming rate.

Ferryman was leaning over to kiss Keira when one of the guards sounded the village horn to alert everyone that they were under attack.

Hideous calls could be heard as the troll army closed in on the village.

"We're under attack! Come with me," Ferryman grabbed Keira's hand and they ran off.

The villagers were panic-stricken. They screamed in horror as they scrambled to find their kin. Captain Darak Kilgorn of the king's guard sounded his horn to call his men to arms.

Captain Kilgorn raced to find King Roland.

"Sire, an army of trolls lay siege to our village," he exclaimed.

"Trolls? I thought we rid the land of those foul creatures long ago," said King Roland.

"No doubt Gelda, the Elven witch has been busy breeding them," replied Pantul.

"Captain, send the signal to escape to the forest."

Captain Kilgorn blew his horn several times. People were running around grabbing what belongings they could carry and heading toward the castle where a secret passageway way led to the sanctuary of the Greenhorn Forest. King Roland saw Ferryman and Keira running across the courtyard.

"Ferryman, come here," shouted King Roland.

Ferryman and Keira ran over to him.

Pantul handed Ferryman the White Book of Magic. "Keep the book safe. If you happen to misplace the book listen for the book's song and it will lead you to it."

Queen Errisa gave Ferryman a leather satchel to put the book in. King Roland hands Ferryman a spear and a horn.

"You're a man now Ferryman. Here's my father's spear and horn. Now take your mother and the others to safety." King Roland looked Ferryman straight in his eyes.

Ferryman proudly took the spear and horn from his father. It was a moment that Ferryman had looked forward to for a long time. "I'll protect them with my life." The king and his son embraced.

Keira's father ran over to Keira and hugged her.

The Troll King and his army stopped just before reaching the village gate. Soldiers aligned the village wall staring down at the trolls that were wailing and waving their weapons. The Troll King pointed his scepter at the village gate. A powerful bolt of green lightning leaped from the scepter, striking the village gate, which exploded in green flames and killed many of those who stood upon the wall. The trolls immediately rushed the gate and were met by the king's army. One of the guards sounded a horn signaling that the village gate had been breached. "The gate has been breached!" he shouted.

The king ordered the servants to only take two wooden chests for him and his wife. They carried chests off into the passageway.

King Roland hugged his wife. "Take the passageway to the forest. I'll join you later," said the king as Queen Errisa squeezed her husband's hand. "Go now."

Ferryman tugged at Keira's hand, but she didn't want to go.

"Go with them, my daughter," said Keira's father.

"No. I won't leave you," screamed Keira.

"Do as you're told, daughter. I can't fight and worry about you at the same time."

Ferryman led her away with his mother and others into the passageway so they could escape to the Greenhorn Forest.

King Roland, Captain Kilgorn, Pantul, and others mounted horses and galloped off to meet the enemy. They arrived at the gate where the king's army was fighting to hold back the invading trolls. The Troll King and his army crashed through the flaming walls of the gate. The armies clashed in a bloody and violent fervor. Pantul shot several fireballs into the heart of the troll army, killing several of them. It was to no avail as the Troll King fired his scepter at Pantul knocking him off his horse. The Troll King eyed King Roland and swatted him off his horse. As the Troll King was about to crush the king's skull Keira's father tried to stop the Troll King but was killed by a single blow.

Ferryman and Keira walked hand in hand through the Greenhorn Forest along with other survivors from the onslaught when two trolls appeared out of nowhere.

"Trolls! Run!" shouted Ferryman.

Keira stood her ground, picked up a rock, loaded her rock shooter, commonly known as a slingshot, and shot one of the trolls in the face.

"Take that you wretched creature," she yelled.

The troll screamed and made a beeline for Keira. Ferryman jumped in front of her. "Keira. Run." But he was swatted away. The troll grabbed Keira and both trolls ran off into the forest. Ferryman got back onto his feet with his nasty shiner thumping. Ferryman handed the leather satchel to his mother, grabbed his spear and horn, and chased after Keira.

Pantul shot a fireball that hit the Troll King in the face, distracting him long enough to pull the King to safety.

The village was overrun. Many Elven and men folk lay dead or dying in the village streets as flames rose up from the buildings, lighting up the night sky. Pantul launched a red fireball into the air signaling a call to retreat. "Retreat! The village is lost!"

A guard saw the signal and blew the horn signaling that the village had fallen. A troll killed him shortly afterward.

*

Gelda laughed as she watched the events unfolding in the seeing orb.

Pantul, Captain Kilgorn, King Roland, and the remaining survivors of the king's army retreated into the king's castle and barricaded the entrance to allow time for everyone to escape through the passageway leading to the forest. Pantul stayed behind and guarded the entrance as everyone fled. "Go, I won't be far behind," shouted Pantul. The trolls smashed through the barricade. With the trolls hot on his heels, he shot a barrage of fireballs at them as he disappeared down the passageway. Pantul then collapsed the tunnel behind him killing the trolls who followed and completely blocking the passageway.

Ferryman ran as fast as he could through the forest. The two trolls and Keira were just up ahead of him. He could hear Keira screaming for help. "Put me down you foul piece of horse dung!" Keira bit the troll, forcing it to drop her on the ground. She immediately got up and ran. The troll gave chase as Ferryman charged it with a spear, piercing the troll in its eye and killing it. The other troll attacked Ferryman, slicing him across his chest with his claw. Ferryman fell to the ground, bleeding profusely, and fell unconscious. Keira picked up the spear and swung at the troll, slashing its eye. The troll screamed and ran away.

Keira ran over to Ferryman. "No, don't die," cried Keira as tears ran down her cheek. Keira blew Ferryman's horn and others came to their aid. Ferryman was carried back to camp.

Pantul emerged from the secret passageway into the forest and headed toward the encampment. He soon caught up with the other survivors. Everyone who survived the attack watched the roaring flames rising up through the night sky as the village burned. The wounded were many and there were few horses left. They hung their heads as they headed off into the night.

Outside the burning village, the trolls celebrated their victory. The Troll King took a bite out of a giant Eglort drumstick and then took a gulp of ale, he grunted with pleasure, and in the excitement, his scepter erupted and blew up a big fat troll hurling his green flaming guts all over the place. All the trolls stopped for a brief moment and then burst out into laughter as they continued their celebration. They feasted on the Eglort and drank mugs of ale throughout the night.

Queen Errisa was tending Roland's wounds when Pantul arrived. Keira was patting Ferryman's forehead with a damp cloth as Ferryman lay with his chest bandaged.

"Sire, we are safe for the time being, but we should seek aide from Windor," said Pantul.

"Yes, let us first tend to our wounded," replied King Roland.

Keira looked around in a panic. "Where is my father?"

"Your father was very brave. He gave his life to save mine. You should be proud of him," King Roland told her gravely.

Keira started crying. Ferryman woke up and squeezed her hand.

"It's going to be all right," said Ferryman.

"What's going to happen to me? He was the only family I have left," cried Keira.

"We're your family now. We'll take care of you." Ferryman held her close.

*

Gelda watched the village burn in her seeing orb. She saw King Roland and the others making their way through the Forest.

"Take my father from me and I take everything from you," Gelda said. She looked at her servant. She laughed.

The Troll King listened intently to Gelda as she spoke from the orb. "Take the army and pursue King Roland. Pray they don't escape again." The Troll King grunted acknowledging her command. The Troll King called the other trolls to arms and they ran off into Greenhorn Forest.

King Roland, Queen Errisa, Captain Kilgorn, and Pantul led the survivors through the forest on horseback. A bluebird lands on Pantul's shoulder and chirps. "Thank you, my friend. Sire, the troll army still pursues us. We are a few days ahead of them."

King Roland maneuvered next to Captain Kilgorn. "Captain dispatch your fastest rider to Windor. We are in need of their help. With luck, the troll army won't catch up to us before they arrive."

Pantul looked back at the king. "Sire, it's best if we head to River Forks Plain. It's halfway to Windor. We just have to be careful. There are many dangers in the forest."

The bluebird chirped at Pantul again. "Goodbye, little Perry." The bluebird flew away.

Captain Kilgorn rode off to his soldiers. Ferryman and Keira rode side by side. Ferryman looked at Keira. "Are you ok?"

Keira smiled at him. "I'll survive. I'm not so fragile you know."

Ferryman laughed," Good thing."

"Let us make haste to Windor," said King Roland.

"The witch's troll army will pursue us," said Pantul.

"Captain, dispatch your fastest rider to Windor. We are in need of their army. With luck the Troll army won't catch up to us before they arrive," said King Roland.

"It's best if we head to River Fork Plain. There we can meet up with King Eland and his army," replied Pantul.

Pantul looked around at the ground. "We'll let the rain wash away our tracks." Pantul waved his staff and uttered the incantation, "Tinlor prentra disov." Thunderstorm clouds suddenly rolled in releasing rain. Pantul looked straight up into the clouds letting the rain hit his face. "With luck, the troll army won't find us. At least for a while."

The rain washed away any trace of their presence and the glow of the burning village lit up the distant sky as they made their way to River Fork Plain.

Chapter 2

The Horn of the Sea

The splendor that is Windor, the city by the sea, glistened with gold, silver, steel, and crystal that illuminated with the colors of the rainbow as the rider, Marin, an Elven girl in her twenties, approached. She was dwarfed in comparison to the size of the city gates as her horse gallantly galloped like a well-oiled machine with a most desperate plea. A sweet cherry fragrance graced her nostrils as she rode along a dirt path lined with blossoming cherry trees growing in a meadow filled with tall green grass and colorful flowers. She blew her horn and the mammoth city gates slowly opened allowing her to enter the inner sanctum.

The Elven King Aron Turin and his Elven wife Queen Arien sat on their thrones in the Hall of Windor, a sanctum in the king's palace where the people could gather to bring grievances or make merriment. The minstrels were playing a happy Elven love song as couples pranced about. Other couples were eating slices of a roasted horned beast and drinking Elven Green Ale. When the king's guard and Marin entered the hall, the king raised his hand. The music instantly stopped, and everyone fell silent, all eyes on the newcomer.

Marin and the king's guard strolled toward the king's throne. The smell of roasted Eglort filled the hall. It made her mouth water. When they stopped Marin removed her helmet and she bowed. "Sire, a rider from King Roland seeks an audience."

The king signaled for Marin to rise. Marin stepped forward. "Sire, I come with ill tidings of the fall of Beldredor. An army of trolls invaded and burned the village to the ground."

King Aron rose from his throne. "Gelda is surely behind this attack. It's been so long since her banishment."

"King Roland requests that you meet him at River Forks Plain as soon as possible."

"Tell King Roland we will see him soon. Guard! Sound the Horn of the Sea. Let us ride out and drive the vermin from our neighbor's land."

The king's guard hurried off to pass the order of the king along to the tower where the Great Horn of the Sea was situated.

The horn blasted so loudly that everyone in Windor had to cover their ears and it could be heard throughout the land as far as the Black Mountains.

King Roland and the other survivors were camping in the Greenhorn Forest when they heard the sound that help was on its way.

"Sh! Listen! The sweet sound of the Horn of the Sea," Pantul announced.

Everyone cheered.

Beloche the Troll King and his army were alarmed as they marched through the Greenhorn Forest and stopped dead in their tracts. A few of the trolls were frightened and tried to run off but the Troll King zapped them with his scepter before they got too far. The Troll King barked his grunts to keep the others in line and pointed his scepter toward their destination and they continued onward.

The sun was high when King Aron and his army rode out of the gates of Windor with dragon banners flapping in the wind.

King Roland and the others soon made camp at the Urot River, at the ford where they had decided to cross. Elven and men folk worked together to cut down trees and build rafts.

King Roland, Pantul, and Captain Kilgorn warmed themselves at a fire, while Ferryman and Keira were busy having fun climbing trees.

Pantul spied a bluebird sitting in a tree and whistled. The bluebird flew down and landed on Pantul's shoulder. The bird chirped then Pantul whispered to it and it flew off.

Pantul was ecstatic as he turned to the others. "It seems we've put some distance between us and the troll army."

Captain Kilgorn looked around at the families and children spread out around the encampment. "That's good news because we're running out of food. We should send out a hunting party while we wait for the rafts to be built."

King Roland looked up at Ferryman. "Yes, take my son with you. It's time for his first hunt. Ferryman, come down here."

"I'll be right down." Ferryman tumbled to the ground with a thump after testing a weak branch. He and Keira ran over to King Roland and the others.

*

Gelda sat in her laboratory reading the Black Book of Magic. "The White Book of Magic can be used in the transference ritual. I will be more powerful than the entire wizard's council."

She threw some old bones onto the ground. She picked up a knife and a cup and glided over to a small wooden cage. When she opened the cage door a small black and white puppy wagged its tail. Grinning from ear to ear she slit the puppy's throat and drained its blood into the cup. She sprinkled the blood on the old bones and read aloud from the Black Book of Magic. "Lupus gravita flestile."

The bones shook and rattled as flesh and fur formed and grew into a pack of wolves. The leader, a large white wolf named Emerrine, and six other smaller wolves as black as coal stood before her with green growing eyes and saliva dripping from their razor-sharp fangs.

The witch had aged ten years. This was the price of her magic. She could see the change in her hands as she barked out her commands. "Young Ferryman carries the White Book of Magic. It should be easy to get it from him. Kill Ferryman and bring me the book and I will change you into a man."

Emerrine smiled. "Then I will rule the forest." He and the others ran off to complete their mission.

*

Keira was compelled to jump into the hunting conversation. "I want to go with the hunting party."

The king gave her an odd look. "Eglorts are big and ferocious. Only men can go on the hunt."

Ferryman felt bad for Keira. He had come to see the adventurer in her and welcomed her company. He handed her the satchel that held the White Book of Magic. "Will you hold on to the book for me, so I won't lose it?"

Keira smiled as she slung it over her shoulder. "Sure."

Captain Kilgorn and six others rode up. Captain Kilgorn was leading a black stallion behind him for Ferryman. "Are you ready, lad?"

Ferryman climbed up onto the horse then King Roland handed him his spear. "Mind your wits, son, and you'll be all right."

Pantul stood watching. "Perhaps I should go along."

The king thought for a moment. "I'd rather you'd stay with the woman and children."

Captain Kilgorn pulled his horse around. "I'll stay close to him."

The hunting party rode off with high expectations of feasting on roasted Eglort. Ferryman looked back to see his mother standing next to Keira, waving. He waved back as he rode off.

*

Gelda spied the Troll King in her seeing orb. "King Aron rides west then south. King Roland is moving toward the northwest. They must be heading for River Forks Plain and you'll be waiting for them."

The Troll King acknowledged with grunts, raised his scepter, and pointed it in the direction the Troll army would be traveling. The seeing orb grew dark as the troll army ran off.

*

Keira was not about to be left out of the hunt, so she followed the hunting party on horseback, being careful not to be seen. Ferryman looked back occasionally but saw nothing.

Emerrine and the wolfpack stopped for a moment. Emerrine could smell them. He knew they were close. "Spread out." They all ran off in different directions.

As the evening began to fade to darkness, the hunting party made camp. Growling stomachs could be heard as the aroma of rabbits roasted over the campfire drifted on the wind.

Keira was not far off, watching from a distance and out of sight, hidden by dense brush.

Captain Kilgorn stood up and drew his sword. "While we're waiting let's see how you handle a sword."

Ferryman pulled out his knife. "This is all I have."

Captain Kilgorn handed him a sword. "You can have this one."

Ferryman was excited. He sliced the air and twirled the blade. "Will you teach me sword fighting?"

Captain Kilgorn drew his sword. "We'll begin with basic fighting stances and guard positions."

Keira was trying to stay awake, but she was so tired that she fell asleep in the brush.

A black wolf that was watching the camp from afar ran off to get the others. The sun was just piercing the darkness when the pack of wolves arrived back at the encampment. The hunting party had moved on. Emerrine could smell them as he sniffed the misty air. "They're not far off." Emerrine and the pack scurried down the dark trail in hot pursuit.

A flock of Eglorts was wandering about in a clearing, feasting on fat little rodents. They were unaware that the hunting party was stalking them. One Eglort wandered close to them. They readied their spears for the kill as Emerrine and the wolfpack moved into position to attack.

Keira saw the wolfpack and signaled the hunting party by blowing her horn. Ferryman and Emerrine immediately turned their attention to her. Ferryman saw the big white wolf run toward Keira. "Keira!" He broke from the hunting party and raced off to help her. The flock of Eglorts was spooked as the pack of wolves attacked the hunting party, killing several hunters. The Eglorts attacked the wolves and hunters, both, in their rampage.

Keira readied her spear as Emerrine charged toward her. Ferryman threw his spear at Emerrine, but it soared over his head. Emerrine turned toward Ferryman who then drew his sword. Emerrine leaped at Ferryman knocking him off his horse and then pounced on Ferryman. Keira screamed and threw her spear, but it missed. As she started to run over to Ferryman an Eglort snatched her up by her collar and made off into the forest. "Let go of me!"

Covered in wolf's blood Ferryman squeezed out from under Emerrine. He pulled his sword out of Emerrine's neck, jumped onto his horse, and gave chase after Keira.

Keira flopped around as the Eglort streaked through the forest. As hard as she tried, she could not break free of the beast's beak. Then suddenly she found herself falling into a large nest and staring down a pair of hungry baby Eglorts as big as she was. She looked up at them. "Oh oh." She drew her knife and slowly rose to her feet. "Easy does it. You don't want to eat me. I'm not very tasty."

Ferryman rode as fast as he could. "Keira. Where are you?" Fortunately, the Eglort tracks were easy to follow. They led him right to the nest. He had just gotten off his horse when the mother Eglort came out of nowhere snapping at him as if he was a tasty rodent. Ferryman shimmied up a tree before the Eglort could eat him. It jumped at him, snapping its razor-sharp beak. Ferryman jumped onto the Eglort's back and stabbed it repeatedly with his sword. The beast ran off wildly making an awful squawking noise. Ferryman kept stabbing the giant beast as he hung on for dear life until the beast finally dropped dead in its tracks. Ferryman caught his breath and ran as fast as he could back to the nest. He jumped into the nest only to find Keira bloodied with bite marks, trying to fend off the baby creatures. Without hesitation, he cut both of the baby Eglorts' heads off. Keira jumped into Ferryman's arms. He looked her straight in her baby blue eyes. "That was close. You all right?" She nodded as they kissed. They climbed out of the nest and Ferryman blew his horn so the others could find them.

Captain Kilgorn and three others soon arrived on horseback. Ferryman waved. "Where are the others? I've slain an Eglort for our feast."

Captain Kilgorn slid down off his horse. He looked at Keira. "They didn't make it, but neither did the wolf pack. We all might be dead if you hadn't warned us."

She sheathed her knife. "Just doing my duty, sire."

Ferryman gave Keira a big squeeze. "Captain, I want to bring back the white wolf's carcass to skin and burn for the festival of the wolf."

Captain Kilgorn nodded in agreement but didn't look too happy about it. "Well, we'll need some sleds to drag the beasts back to camp. That means cutting down some trees unless you have a magic spell handy."

Ferryman didn't know what to say in response, so he just shook his head.

After constructing the sleds, they buried their friends and then made off with the beasts in tow.

They were cheered by the others as they rode into camp. The cook ran right to the Eglort and sized it up for the spit. Queen Errisa examined the large white wolf. "This will make a fine cloak for you, my son. There's enough fur for boots as well." Then she embraced him.

The king stood by grinning from ear to ear with pride that his son had become a man and killed his first Eglort with the very spear with which he had made his first kill when he was a lad. "Skin the beasts and prepare them for the festival. I wish we had some cake and ale but roasted Eglort sounds mighty tasty."

Pantul strolled up mumbling to a bluebird that was perched on his shoulder. "Sire, I'm told the troll army is no longer following us."

This was good news for the king, but it puzzled him. "Where did they go?"

The bluebird chirped as if answering the king's question. They all looked at Pantul, waiting for his wisdom. "I'm not entirely sure but I suspect they are headed for River Fork Plain."

The king looked around at all the curious faces surrounding him. "They mean to ambush us, but they'll have to wait for us to get there. Tomorrow we cross the river. So, let the festival of the wolf begin."

The king embraced his son as everyone cheered. "Come, tell me all about your adventure." They strolled off as father and son.

The queen took Keira's hand. "Let's get you bandaged up."

It was a jubilant night as the Eglort roasted over the open spit. The folks danced as the minstrels played. Pantul was busy showing off his miniature fireworks for the children. Ferryman and Keira slowly danced as they gazed into each other's eyes. Captain Kilgorn tapped Ferryman on the shoulder. "May I dance with this brave young woman?"

Ferryman yielded. "By all means, Captain."

Ferryman strolled over to Pantul. "Well Ferryman, have you been studying the book?"

"Yes. It's told me some fascinating tales of the old days."

Pantul shook his head. "Good. Now you need to ask a question. Place your right hand on it and ask. When you open it, the book will tell you what you need to know."

Ferryman pulled the White Book of Magic out of his satchel and placed his right hand on it. "What should I ask?"

Pantul shook his head. "Ask it anything."

"Will I marry Keira?" He then opened the book and read. "It says, 'The future has many paths.' What does that mean?"

Pantul laughed. "It just means it's up to you and her to decide. When you have a more serious problem to solve it will be more helpful. In the meantime, just keep reading."

"I will. Captain Kilgorn has been training me to sword fight."

"Excellent. Being a wizard means protecting folks. You will need to be strong and cunning."

"It's a big responsibility. I don't want to disappoint anyone."

Pantul put his hand on Ferryman's shoulder. "Just be yourself. In time you will build your confidence. You'll see. I know the responsibility of being a wizard can be overwhelming. But it can be joyous as well. You decide which."

Ferryman looked at his father as he wandered over. "My son the hunter. I couldn't be prouder of you."

Ferryman embraces his father. "Thank you, father. It was quite an adventure." Ferryman looked at Keira as she danced.

King Roland looked at Keira. He saw her looking over at Ferryman. He then turned back to observe Ferryman. "I can tell you two are in love. She's a strong woman. She'll make a fine wife when you're old enough."

The fire builder was busy preparing the spit to roast the Eglort and the bonfire for the wolf's carcass. The king saw him signaling that they were ready. "It's time."

They all gathered around the bonfire. The wolf's skinned carcass was placed on the woodpile. Ferryman was given the honor of lighting the fire. As the fire stirred, they all sang an Elven song to remember their loved ones.

*

Gelda's beastly servant entered her laboratory with a young Elven lad who was bound and gagged. Gelda looked him over as he nervously stood before her. "What do we have here?"

Her servant dared not look at her directly as he spoke. "He was found wandering in the Ont Forest. Maybe he will be of use to you."

Gelda glided over to the Black Book of Magic. "Let's see what the book says." She placed her left hand on the book. "What use is this Elven lad to me?" She looked straight into the eyes of the boy, which sent shivers up and down his spine. She opened the book and read aloud. "It says the young lad can be used in a minor transference ritual. His life energy can restore my youth."

She gazed at her reflection in her mirror. "Bring him here."

Her servant pushed the lad closer to her. She placed her hand on his forehead and read aloud from the Black Book of Magic. "Gravitras Spiritranslo unu impetinum."

The boy's spiritual energy transferred to Gelda leaving him a shriveled-up corpse. After the transference was complete, she discarded the lad as she would a chicken bone, she had just finished gnawing on. She looked at herself in the mirror. "Bring me more young boys."

Her servant stepped back away from her. "We were fortunate to have found him so close to the castle. We would have to go to one of the villages for others. It's risky."

She stared at him with mean eyes. "It's your head, not mine. Bring me another boy or I'll see if you can bring me youth."

Her servant quickly bowed and left her presence.

*

King Roland stood watching the river as it lazily flowed by. The people were boarding a large raft that would be used to cross the river to the other side. A thick vine stretched to the other side of the river so they could pull themselves across.

Pantul was standing next to Ferryman when a bluebird landed on his shoulder and chirped.

Ferryman was curious as to what the bird said. "What did he say?"

Pantul scratched his head. "He says we should be careful crossing the river. Something about river fish."

Ferryman chuckled... "Fish? We'll catch them for dinner."

Ferryman signaled to the bird. It turned its head and flew off. Ferryman was dismayed. "You'll have to teach me the bluebird trick sometime."

Pantul waived as the bird disappeared. "It's not a trick. Little Perry is my friend."

Ferryman was even more curious now. "But how do you understand him?"

"We'll I am a wizard. Aren't I?"

"Well, yes."

"There you have it then."

"Have what?"

"Exactly."

Keira strolled up carrying two sacks filled with her belongings. "I'm here." Queen Errisa followed behind her.

Ferryman looked at her bags. "Where did you get all that stuff?"

Keira clutched her sacks. "They're clothes. Gifts from friends."

Ferryman wasn't about to say anymore.

The king took Queen Errisa by the hand. "My dear, Ferryman, Keira. Climb aboard."

They all stepped aboard the raft. All Ferryman could see on the other side was more forest. "What's on the other side and where are we going from there?"

King Roland steadied himself as the raft rocked. "The Great Seawood Forest, which lies between the Urot River and Windor by the Sea. From there we travel northwest along the Urot River to River Fork Plain."

As the raft was being pulled across a huge fish jumped out of the river and snatched up poor Lennel as he struggled to pull the boat along. Everyone stood still. They could see a school of huge fish swimming toward them. Captain Kilgorn stood ready with his spear. The fish started leaping at them. "Everyone get down!" shouted the Captain as more fish jumped at them.

Pantul raised his staff. "Rinlor Protelicus fieltin forts."

A ring of fire formed around the raft. The fish swam around and stopped jumping at them. Finally, they reached the other side and made camp. King Roland led a vigil for the dead, "They will be missed and remembered for the rest of our days." They all sang a song of remembrance and tossed flowers into the river as the sun gave into the darkness.

Chapter 3

Secrets of Seawood Forest

Gelda paced about her laboratory as she secretly watched Ferryman and company in her seeing orb as they made their way through the forest. Gelda stood gazing into the orb, "They approach Septer's cave. She and her young will be hungry."

Captain Kilgorn led the way as the company passed through the ancient Seawood Forest. Ferryman looked around in wonder. He had never seen trees that towered so high that you would surely fall over trying to look straight up at one. They were so big around. Ferryman pointed to perhaps the biggest tree he'd ever seen. "We could carve a home out of that one."

Pantul pointed to the tree. "That tree is known as Namrehs. It is the King of the Seawood Forest. Sire, we have to be watchful from here on out. We're moving into Septer's realm."

Keira rode up beside Ferryman. "Who is Septer?"

Pantul squinted his left eye and looked right at Keira. "I've never seen it myself you know. I've only heard stories about flesh-eating beasts that live in the caves nearby and have a hearty appetite for young children. They usually stay close to their lair. If we are quiet, we may pass by unnoticed."

Ferryman and Keira looked at each then cautiously looked about.

Keira grabbed Ferryman's hand. "Do you think the beast will try and eat us?"

Ferryman squeezed her hand tightly. "We'll protect you if it does."

They saw skeletons of various animals scattered about. Suddenly two snakes, possibly ten feet in length, slithered out of the brush chasing a rabbit.

Pantul immediately noticed. "Septer's babies. The quicker we get out of these parts the better."

A giant Big Horned Owl swooped down and snatched up one of the baby snakes. The poor creature yelped an unnerving squealing hissing sound as it was carried off in the clutches of the owl's talons.

Septer hissed as her glowing green eyes opened in the darkness of her cave. "Ssssss my baby," she cried.

Ferryman was shocked by the incident and rode off in the direction of the owl. "I'll save it!"

Keira followed behind him. "Wait for me," she cried out.

Pantul was dismayed. "Ferryman, Keira, come back!"

King Roland signed for everyone to stop. Captain Kilgorn quickly volunteered to go after them. "I'll bring them back." He galloped off with a furious fervor.

Ferryman and Keira were trying to keep up with the owl.

The owl descended onto its nest as the baby snake frantically wiggled and hissed, desperately trying to free itself from the owl's talons. Two hungry baby owls squawked in anticipation of the tasty morsel.

Ferryman and Keira stopped at the tree and Ferry dismounted. He looked up at the tree as he prepared to shimmy up.

Keira pulled out a rock slinger to give to Ferryman. "Here take this."

"What is it?"

"Here I'll show you." She bent down and picked up a rock and placed it in the pocket of the slinger. She pulled back the pocket, took aim, and let the rock fly. She handed it to Ferryman. "Thanks. This will come in handy."

Ferryman stuffed a handful of rocks and the rock slinger into his pouch and began climbing as Captain Kilgorn rode up.

Septer saw King Roland and the others and slithered to them. Pantul stood with his staff between Septer and company. Septer hissed at them in anger. "What have you done with my baby?" A multitude of baby snakes began to surround them.

Pantul raised his staff. It was taken by a Great Horned Owl."

They found themselves surrounded by a sea of snakes. The top of Pantul's staff began to glow. "We mean you no harm. We're just passing through."

All the snakes surrounding them hissed and slithered about.

Ferryman looked down as approached the nest. He couldn't see Keira at all. He popped his head above the rim of the nest and pulled out his rock slinger. He loaded it, took aim, and hit the mama owl square between the eyes. Knocked senseless, she fell backward and let go of the baby snake, which fell into the nest. The two baby owls frantically tried to eat it but Ferryman knocked one of the babies out with the rock slinger, giving the baby snake a chance to survive. Ferryman reached in to grab it but it slipped away. "Stupid snake. Come here."

Ferryman grabbed the snake as the baby owl tried to chomp on it. Ferryman wrapped the snake around his neck and climbed down the tree.

Keira was wary of the snake but mustered the courage to pet it. "He's cute."

Captain Kilgorn sidled over to see it. "He's cute until he eats you."

Ferryman held the snake's head up. "Are you sure? I didn't see any people's bones lying around, only animals."

Captain Kilgorn looked the snake in its eyes. "I don't know if the stories are true or not." He reached out his hand to pet the snake. The snake opened its mouth and hissed at him.

Captain Kilgorn cautiously backed away from it. "We'd better get back." They mounted up and rode off.

As they rode up to the others the baby snake squawked. Ferryman dismounted and placed the snake on the ground and it crawled over to its mother and rubbed up against her.

Septer moved closer to Ferryman. "Who must I thank for saving my baby?"

"I'm Ferryman."

"Well Ferryman, if you ever need my help, you know where to find me. Come along children. We don't eat people unless there's nothing else to eat."

The snakes hissed and slithered away.

King Roland raised his hand to get everyone's attention. "We still have daylight left. Let's keep going."

Pantul smiled and pat Ferryman on the shoulder. "You've taught us all a valuable lesson here today. It's time to step up you're training."

Ferryman's eyes widened. "What will you teach me now?"

"First of all, patience. You'll find out when we camp."

They all moved out.

***

Gelda watched Ferryman and others in her seeing orb.

She clenched her fist. "Clever boy. Soon you'll be dead, and the book will be mine."

***

They all rode on until dusk and made camp for the night. After dinner, Ferryman and Keira went off on their own. They sat holding hands while they stargazed. Pantul strolled up and Keira figured they would want to be alone, so she left. "I'm going to see if your mother has finished the wolf fur cloak. I'll be back."

Pantul sat down next to Ferryman. "Ferryman get out the book. I'm going to teach you how to use a wizard's staff. When the time comes the book will show you the steps for making your own staff and sword."

Ferryman took the White Book of Magic out of his satchel. "When will that be?"

"When you're ready. The book will know. Place your right hand on the book." Ferryman placed his right hand on the book. "Ask the question: 'How do I use a wizard's staff?'"

"How do I use a wizard's staff?" repeated Ferryman.

Pantul pointed to the book. "Now open the book and read what it says."

Ferryman opened the book and read," Grasp the staff firmly. Point the end of the staff toward a target of your choosing. Recite the words, 'Illumina numinor.'"

Pantul handed him his staff. Ferryman took the staff and pointed toward a big rock across the way. "Illumina numinor." A fireball shot out of the staff and hit the rock.

Pantul couldn't help but smile. "Excellent. What else does the book say?"

Ferryman looked down. "It says that there are many incantations that can be used depending on the need. Then there is a list of uses and incantations. Here's one. Lightning."

Pantul shook his head. "For some reason, I never get that to work. Every wizard has different abilities."

Again Ferryman pointed the staff at the rock and recited, "Energios irritcuna." Lightning streamed out of the staff and hit the rock causing it to split in half.

Pantul was very pleased with Ferryman. "Very good. You're almost ready."

Ferryman raised his eyebrow at him. "Ready for what?"

Pantul rose to his feet. "When it's time you will have to go off on a long journey. When you have returned you will be a full-fledged wizard if you will. The book will instruct you. For now, keep reading."

***

Gelda spied the Troll king in her seeing orb. "Pantul and the others are almost there. King Aron has been delayed. Allow them to camp and attack at dawn." The orb went dark as she left the laboratory, taking the Black Book of Magic with her. She walked down a winding stone staircase that led to her dungeon. The skeletons chained to the wall were evidence of her heinousness. Rats ran wild, unafraid. She stopped then placed her left hand on the book and spoke aloud, "Batriva gravita flestile."

Several of the rats grew to five times their size. Wings and fangs sprouted out of their furry bodies.

Gelda laughed as they flew all around her. "Go! Fly to River Forks Plain and feast on the flesh of men and Elven folk."

But Gelda paid the price for her use of magic. She aged thirty years in a matter of seconds and looked like a woman in her sixties. She wailed as she eyed the wrinkles on her hands and face. Her screams could be heard well outside the castle as the flying rats raced in a fit of hunger toward their destination.

***

The happy bluebird Perry spotted the Troll King and his army as he perched on a branch. It listened as the witch instructed him. The Troll King was alert to his presence. He fired his scepter at Perry but missed the target. As Perry took flight he was hit by another blast and Perry exploded, scattering his feathers to the wind. The Troll King marveled at his own ingenuity.

***

King Roland and company finally arrived at River Forks Plain. Pantul expected to see Perry the Bluebird. "I wonder where Perry is"

Captain Kilgorn and Pantul rode ahead while the others waited in silence. After a spell, they returned. Captain Kilgorn reported to King Roland. "Sire, there's no sign of King Aron or the Troll army."

Pantul looked around suspiciously. "We're being watched."

"King Roland thought for a moment. "We need to rest for now. We'll set up camp. Have the men keep watch."

The dawn came quickly. The fog had set in. Guards were walking around the camp as the rest slumbered. One of the guards heard wings flapping overhead. He looked up and could only see silhouettes of flying creatures circling the campsite.

The Troll King and his army emerged from the darkness. Grunting. Wailing. The guards perked up as the sound of thunder approached. The morning sun soon revealed the Troll King and his army barreling toward the encampment. The guards immediately sounded their horns to alert everyone of the impending danger. Everyone jumped up and scrambled for their lives. Anyone who could wield a weapon grabbed one and formed a barrier around the women and children. Captain Kilgorn, King Roland, Pantul, and some of his men met the enemy on horseback. The Troll King's army outnumbered King Roland and company and they had them completely boxed in. Captain Kilgorn sat tall in his saddle, "Sire, they have us surrounded."

Ferryman and Keira held each other tightly. Queen Errisa stepped in front of them to keep them safe.

The Troll King grunted as he pointed to Pantul. The rest of the Troll army grunted and made hideous noises while they jumped up and down. Pantul raised his staff in defense. "Rinlor Protelicus fieltin forrts."

Fire flowed out of the staff creating a wall of fire between them and the Troll army. A few of the Trolls caught fire and ran about screaming. This enraged the Troll King, and he jumped through the wall of fire and fired his scepter at Pantul. The green lightning hit Pantul in the chest sending him flying to the ground. The firewall died and some Trolls ran through and attacked. Captain Kilgorn and his men met them head-on. Captain Kilgorn chopped the head off the first Troll he encountered. "Protect the women and children!" They rode to meet the other Trolls with their swords in their hands.

Pantul got up and the wall of fire strengthened. The Troll King moved toward the women and children killing several soldiers in the process. He then attacked Pantul again. Pantul shot several fireballs at the Troll King, but he was able to brush them off. He blasted Pantul again with his scepter. Pantul was stunned and knocked to the ground. The wall of fire dissipated allowing the flying rats to attack as well. Archers shot at them relentlessly, but they kept coming, they aimed for the neck. The Troll King's rampage became a killing frenzy as anything that got in his way was pulverized.

Pantul lay on the ground, hurt and weak. He mustered up enough strength to stand and utter the incantation, "Protelicus fieltin poofneti." Streams of fire ascended into the air forming a fireball that exploded in the midst of the swarm of flying rats killing most of them.

The Troll King blasted Pantul again with his scepter. His staff flew out of his hand as he tumbled to the ground. Ferryman ran to him. Pantul's chest was badly burned and smoking when he took hold of his hand and leaned over to hear him speak. Pantul struggled as he spoke, "Trust the book. Stay true to yourself." Ferryman had tears in his eyes. "You never taught me the bluebird trick."

With his last breath, Pantul uttered, "Just whistle and it will come." His eyes closed and he died. Ferryman was beside himself as he wiped away the tears. He focused and then grabbed Pantul's staff as the fighting continued all around him.

He saw Keira taking potshots at the Troll King with a rock slinger. The Troll King headed toward her. He pointed his scepter at her.

Ferryman pointed his staff at the Troll King, "No! Energios irritcuna."

A bolt of lightning hit the Troll King sending him flying through the air. The Troll King fired his scepter just as Ferryman shot lighting at him. The two energy streams meet in the center. They pushed each other back and forth testing each other's power. Keira shot the Troll King in the eye with a rock, distracting him long enough for Ferryman to fire at him. The lightning hit the Troll King's scepter, destroying it and badly wounding him.

Ferryman ran over to Keira. They embraced and looked around at the soldiers that were killed. Captain Kilgorn and King Roland lay motionless on the ground. The remaining Troll army slowly moved in to wipe out the rest as the long-awaited horn blasted.

King Aron and his army emerged from the forest in a thundering gallop. Ferryman kept blasting the Trolls with the staff until it got so hot, he couldn't hold it any longer. He dodged a Troll that tried to hack him up and ran away as King Aron and his men overran the encampment and killed or drove off the remaining Troll army. Some of his men chased the Troll King and even though it was badly wounded it managed to disappear into the forest.

Ferryman leaned down to pick up Pantul's staff, but it crumbled into dust. The only thing left to do was console his mother and Keira. Captain Kilgorn and King Roland limped over to join them. He looked over at Pantul and then embraced his wife and Ferryman.

King Aron threw a spear into the back of a Troll trying to run off and rode over to King Roland. After dismounting they shook hands.

King Roland smiled. "Thank you for coming to our aid."

"I wish I had gotten here sooner."

King Roland grabbed Ferryman and put his arm around him. "This is my son. Ferryman."

"The first wizard born in Urot. You saved a lot of lives today, lad."

Ferryman shook his head and put his arm around Keira.

King Aron put his hand on Ferryman's shoulder. "Let us burn the dead and we'll escort you to Windor."

As the sun was setting, they lit the funeral pyre and sent Pantul's body to the wind. Everyone stood before the body singing an ancient Elven song of a wizard's passing. Ferryman wept as he tossed flowers on the fire. "Goodbye, old friend."

***

Gelda was furious that her minions had failed to retrieve the book for her. She was so mad she threw her servant out her window to the rocks below.

***

Ferryman was clutching the satchel that contained the White Book of Magic. Keira hugged him and King Roland hugged Errisa as they watched the fire. They remembered lost companions, all those who had sacrificed their lives so that they would live to pass their memories on to generations to come.

They soon stood before the towering gates of Windor, the city by the sea where anything is possible.

Bonus Story 1

Ferryman's Hunting Trip

Ferryman was excited that he was old enough to go with the hunting party. He spent weeks forging his new sword, pounding and heating it carefully, skillfully until it was fit for a prince. He tested the blade with a small white feather that he floated down through the air, delicately slicing it in two as it drifted. He carefully bound the handle with straps made of the hide of the horned beast and engraved the ancient Elven runes of the hunter upon it.

He greeted his father, King Drakorne, as he stood before the great fireplace staring at the dancing flames.

"Father, I'm ready for the hunt tomorrow. My new sword is finished," said Ferryman.

"Well, let me have a look." His father sliced the air several times observing the balance and craftsmanship.

"A fine sword indeed it is my son. You will have to forge one for me. Now let's go eat. Your mother has prepared a special feast to celebrate your birthday. Roasted horned beast," said his father.

"Hmm, can I carve it?" Ferryman asked.

"Yes, by all means." The King smiled.

They entered the eating hall and to Ferryman's surprise Keira and her father were waiting for them. A bountiful meal was spread out before them. Ferryman salivated as he carefully sliced off portions for everyone. They ate, drank some ale, and sang happy Elven songs while Keira played the harp. Ferryman's mother quietly slipped away and returned with a cherry nut cake with vanilla frosting and thirteen candles. She lit the candles as they sang a birthday wish. Ferryman blew out the candles and cut the cake.

"Here is a gift that I made for you."

His mother kissed him and gave him a sheath for his sword. He strapped it around his waist.

"This is my gift for you," his father said as he handed him a long rolled-up piece of horned beast hide.

Ferryman rolled it open and to his amazement found his father's spear that he used on his first hunting trip.

"As my father passed it down to me, I now pass it on to you," his father said, smiling.

"This is the spear you killed the Eglort with. Maybe I will be as fortunate as you were." Ferryman balanced the spear on his shoulder.

"It would be a treat indeed if you killed an Eglort for the winter village feast," his father said.

Keira gave Ferryman a lock of her hair and a kiss, which made Ferryman blush. Keira's father gave him a dagger that he made when he was young.

"Perhaps this will come in handy on the trail," he said.

"Wonderful gifts from those who are special to me make my birthday very special indeed," said Ferryman.

They all raised their cups and toasted the evening of friendship. Keira and Ferryman slipped away to the garden but not before Ferryman grabbed his sword and sheathed it. Now he felt like an elder.

The moon was bright and reflected its light off the snow in the distance as they held hands.

The morning came quickly as Ferryman rode off on his black stallion. Keira was up early as well and watched him from a distance. She wasn't permitted to accompany the hunting party but that wasn't going to stop her from following them from a distance.

The snow was falling as the hunting party of eight led by Darak Kilgorn, the captain of the king's guard, rode off toward the Ont Forest in the south.

Gelda, the Elven witch of the Black Mountains, stood in her dark chamber, watching them in her seeing crystal orb.

"Yes, go to the forest young Ferryman. My servants are hungry for your flesh," she said as she tossed some bones on the ground.

Gelda placed her hand on the Black Book of Magic and asked the book for an incantation to change the bones into a pack of large wolves. She opened the book and read aloud, "Orhuk troslin lendrontu pentara bankor."

The bones vibrated and multiplied as they formed the skeletons of wolves. Flesh quickly formed around the bones followed by a thick coat of fur. Seven large wolves stood nearly four feet high at the shoulder with eyes that were as red as blood. Six of them were black as coal and the leader was as white as snow.

She spoke to Emerrine the leader while the others paced about.

"Away with all of you to the forest to feast on the Elven folk and men."

"I will eat the flesh of the young wizard myself," Emerrine said as saliva dripped from his mouth.

Emerrine howled and to the hunt they went.

The hunting party reached the forest that was blanketed with snow. Darak signaled to halt when he saw what resembled giant turkey tracks in the snow.

"Eglort tracks. Ferryman, you will come with me. The rest spread out and be watchful so none of you become the Eglort's prey. Use your horn if you eye the beast," Darak said.

The hunting party traveled in pairs stalking the beast. Keira watched them, being careful not to be discovered.

Emerrine and the pack of wolves, hidden by dense brush, observed the party splitting up. The wolves moved in closer waiting for the right moment to strike.

A horn blasted as the Eglort was spotted. The hunters converged on the beast. Keira saw the wolves running after the hunters, so she sounded her horn trying to warn the others. Ferryman knew that it was Keira's horn, so he immediately rode to her aid. Emerrine in the meantime turned his attention toward Keira and Darak rode off to help kill the Eglort.

The wolves attacked the hunters and the Eglort ran off. The hunters fought the wolves as Emerrine attacked Keira knocking her off her horse. Ferryman saw that Keira was in trouble and threw his spear at Emerrine but missed. Emerrine turned his attention to Ferryman. The white wolf leaped through the air onto Ferryman and his horse sending both of them to the ground.

Darak and the other hunters fought bravely but two of them were killed by the surprise attack. Darak killed three of the wolves with his bow and arrows. The other three wolves severely wounded two others before the hunters killed them.

Ferryman drew his sword and ran over to Keira. The white wolf crept toward him, his breath steaming in the cold air.

"Now I will eat you and the girl," Emerrine said.

"How is it that you can speak?" Ferryman said.

"It doesn't matter," Emerrine said as he crept toward them.

Ferryman and Keira backed up. The wolf leaped into the air and Ferryman tripped and fell to the ground as he tried to get out of his way. His sword pierced the wolf in the throat and the beast died. Ferryman was trapped underneath the beast. Keira tried to pull him out but to no avail. She sounded her horn, and the others came to help.

The party left the forest with their dead and the carcass of the white wolf. The wolf was skinned, and Ferryman's mother made him a hooded cloak and boots from the wolf's fur. Even though he could not fit into the garments now, he knew he would one day grow into them.

The dead were honored, and Ferryman's father celebrated his son becoming an elder.

The End

Bonus Story 2

The Wizard's Festival

Beldre woke in the midst of his princely familiarities at sunrise. The sweet scent of cherry and apple blossoms in full bloom brought his senses back to life. Being 17 and the son of a king had its burdens and responsibilities, but that day was a special day for the whole kingdom. It was the day that Ferryman the wizard was returning from his adventures. Beldre was especially excited. It was his birthday, and it was time for the wizard's apprentice to be chosen. He was among five who were born that day, seventeen years ago, the day of the total eclipse and the great comet that lit up the land. It was the sign that a wizard had been born.

The aroma of roasted seasoned meat, music, and laughter brought the kings of the land to King Marcus Drakorne's castle for the wizard's festival. Everyone, especially the children, looked forward to Ferryman's tales and of course the magical fireworks that only a wizard could conjure.

The gathering was magical as elves and menfolk, both kings and peasants, ate and danced in merriment to their heart's content.

The King's family, Ferryman, and the families of the kings of the realm were seated on a large platform overlooking the festival. The fire breathers, jugglers, and dancers' performances thrilled everyone. King Marcus stood up to make a toast. "Here's to my fellow kings of Urot, my good friend, wise counselor, and kinsman, Ferryman the Wizard of Urot."

"Here! Here!" the crowd shouted.

Ferryman stood up in his white wolf-skin cloak and boots. His long white beard and hair swayed in the wind. With his staff of Rume held tightly in his grasp and his sword, Aridun, sheathed he stepped up to greet the crowd.

"Gather the children around and Ferryman will tell one of his adventure tales," said King Marcus.

Ferryman smiled, "Thank you all for the warm welcome. It's good to be among friends." He thought for a moment as everyone waited in anticipation.

"The story I will share with you is about my recent venture into the heart of the Dark Caverns. I was trapped there, in the labyrinth that lies northeast of the mountains of Urot."

Everyone was silent and intently listened as he told his tale of wizardry and magic. "There I was face to face with the creature, Septer the Colossal; a gargantuan snake conjured by the elven witch of the Black Mountains."

The children gripped their parents with their eyes open as wide as could be.

The story ended with a cheer from the crowd. The menacing snake of the Dark Caverns would not be preying on them anymore. The wizard once again proved himself to be a hero to the folks of Urot and the royal families.

One of the menfolk stepped forward to speak his mind. "What of the rumors of the stirrings about at the Black Castle? It is said that the witch and the young wizard Allenel have formed an alliance. We should have killed that wretched creature when we had the chance."

Ferryman replied, "It is written by the wizard council of Eonor that the Elven shall not kill the Elven. Allenel was exiled according to our laws. He has escaped his solitude and now resides with Gelda the witch of the Black

Mountains. Let us defer this discussion for another time. After all, we are here to celebrate the selection of the wizard's apprentice. Let's enjoy ourselves."

"Here! Here!" cheered the crowd.

The merriment of the festival consumed everyone. They laughed as they danced to the music, ate and drank well into the day.

A few hours passed when Ferryman stood up to speak. "Tomlin Cheavers, Jeret Brohan, Pompe Lortu, Roham Kratis and Prince Beldre Drakorne come up here so we can all wish you a happy birthday."

The young men came forward and greeted Ferryman. A large cake was brought out on a cart pulled by an old mule. The cake was so large that it had to be taken off the cart by four strong men. It had three layers coated with white icing, cherries, and nuts. The children stared at the cake in awe with their eyes and mouths as wide open as they could manage. They couldn't wait to devour the luscious treat.

The crowd toasted the young men, raising their glasses and shouting, "Happy birthday!"

They merrily drank and ate cake as Ferryman told the story of his seventeenth birthday.

"It has been nine hundred and some years since I was chosen. I was the first after ten thousand years. It was a grand festival and I remember a cake dripping with blackberry and cherry sauce." He looked right at the children standing near him, smiled, and winked. "As written by the wizard council of Eonor, the wizard's apprentice will be decided by the reading of the Book of White Magic. Only a wizard can read the sacred book. It is the book that chooses the wizard." He looked at the five young men. Pointing his finger he said," One or all of you will be able to read from the book. Then we shall see who is chosen."

The crowd cheered, "The wizard's apprentice!" they raised their glasses and drank.

Princess Errisa came over to Beldre. "I brought you cake," she said, looking straight into his eyes.

"Thank you, Errisa. I was going to bring you some."

They both laughed and talked as they ate their cake. Errisa insisted on dancing. Beldre was happy to accommodate her. She was the love of his life.

Beldre went to get some drinks. He heard a familiar song in his head but not being played by the minstrels. He had heard this song many times throughout his life and wondered where it came from. He felt as if the song was calling to him so he followed his feelings which led him to a tent off the courtyard. Inside was a white book sitting on the table. It seemed to Beldre that the song was coming from the book, which puzzled him. He read the title, "The White Book of Magic, Written by the Wizard Council of Eonor in the First Age."

He didn't dare touch the book. He knew he shouldn't even be looking at it but he couldn't help himself. He was startled by Ferryman.

"You couldn't stay away I see," said Ferryman as he raised his eyebrows. "You hear the song call to you?"

"Yes, I've heard it many times throughout my life," replied Beldre. "I never knew what it was."

Ferryman put his hand on Beldre's shoulder, "I heard the song as well when I was young." Ferryman picked up the book and walked toward the door. "The time has come."

Beldre stared at Ferryman, got up, and headed out the door with him. He was filled with anticipation. He couldn't wait to be called upon to read from the book.

Ferryman stepped onto the platform, and everyone became silent. They knew that it was time to reveal the wizard's apprentice.

Ferryman cleared his throat. "It's time for the reading of the White Book of Magic. We will begin with Tomlin. Come up here and introduce yourself."

The crowd cheered as Tomlin jumped with excitement and ran up to the platform, "Hello. I'm Tomlin Cheavers of the House of Cheavers along the river east of Beldredor. I've been a carpenter's apprentice and cabin boy as long as I can remember."

"Open the book and read what it says," spoke Ferryman.

Tomlin opened the book and to his surprise the pages were blank. He looked at page after page. They were all blank. He said puzzled, "I don't see any writing."

"I'm sorry Tomlin. You have not been chosen," Ferryman said consolingly. The crowd sighed.

Tomlin hung his head and walked off the platform back to his family.

"Pompe Lortu. It's your turn," said Ferryman waiving him to the platform.

The crowd cheered as Pompe went up to the platform.

"Hello everybody. My name is Pompe Lortu." Laughing, "We don't have a house or anything. We live in the caves at the foot of the mountains. I've been working as a chef's apprentice since I was eight years old and burned down the old woodshed."

"Cookin' is women's work," said a snotty kid and all the children laughed.

"Laugh now but when you're older and you're in the midst of fighting the Troll army and the taste of blood and muck sickens your stomach you will come to me to get your rations in gratitude."

"It takes a girl to do a woman's work," the kid yelled, and the rest of the kids laughed aloud.

"Ha! Ha! At least I don't prune flowers."

"I'm a gardener," said the kid defensively.

"Yea, a flower gardener. What kind of woman's work is that?" exclaimed Pompe.

The kids laughed and the snotty kid hung his head and shut up.

"Now! Now! That's enough. Read from the book," Ferryman said with scorn in his voice.

Pompe opened the book as everyone took a deep breath. "There's nothing here!" he cried.

"I'm sorry Pompe, but you have not been chosen," Ferryman said solemnly.

Pompe wiped his tears and went back to his family to be consoled.

"Jeret Brohan. Please come forward," Ferryman called out. The crowd cheered as Jeret stepped forward for his turn.

"Hi. My name is Jeret Brohan. My family lives at a cottage farm at the edge of Windor. We are farmers and it is advantageous to be able to sell crops to the folk of Beldredor and Windor without having to travel great distances."

"I've known your family for a long time. Your farm supplies some of the finest crops around. Very tasty," Ferryman said enthusiastically. "I especially love your berry pies." The crowd stared at Ferryman. "Oh! Sorry, I was lost in the heavenly scent of freshly baked berry pie. How delicious. Please continue."

As Jeret opened the book everyone saw the look of disappointment on his face as he walked off the platform. The crowd sighed.

"Roham Kratis, come forward," said Ferryman.

Roham was born of the Elven folk that lived atop the Mountains of Urot. Even though he only stood nearly three feet tall, he walked with great confidence as he made his way to the platform.

"Greetings to all. My name is Roham Kratis of the Booridan. I have been given the duty of preserving the ancient art of metallurgy. My ancestors mastered this art and forged the noble crowns of Urot signifying the alliance between men and Elven folk after the Great War against the Trolls.

Roham opened the book and alas the pages were blank. He gave the crowd a sad look of disappointment but held his head high as he exited the platform. The crowd sighed.

"Prince Beldre Drakorne, I believe it's your turn," Ferryman said with a smile.

Beldre was nervous and his palms began to sweat. He rubbed them together and blew on them. He gathered his composure and went up to the platform. The crowd was silent. All their hopes of a successor to Ferryman were focused on Beldre, knowing that he was the last and if he failed the test then an apprentice would not be chosen; they would have to wait for others to be born.

"Hello all. My name is Prince Beldre Drakorne and I have worked for many years as a blacksmith's apprentice.

Ferryman briefly remembered his days as the blacksmith's apprentice. He began to stroke his white beard and mustache.

Beldre stared at the book on the podium in front of him. He looked over at his father, King Marcus, who smiled with a nod. He could hear the song loud and clear in his mind. As he opened the book the song stopped. He was shocked as he looked down to read the page. For a moment he stood there silent, which pushed the crowd to the edge of their wits. Then he began to read: "In the year fifteen hundred and twelve of the second age of the Wizard Council of Eonor, I, Prince Beldre Drakorne, have been chosen as the wizard's apprentice as granted by the Wizard Council of Eonor and the Book of White Magic at the beginning of the first age."

Everyone began to shout, "Hail Beldre, the wizard's apprentice!"

King Marcus began shaking hands with the other kings. "That's my son, the great wizard Beldre."

Then they all raised their glasses and drank. The king went over to congratulate his son.

They embraced, both brimming with joy. Beldre's mother, Queen Arien the elven princess of Windor, gently kissed him on his forehead, "I felt the day you were born that you were special. I'm very happy for you, my son." They both smiled as they embraced.

Ferryman walked over to Beldre, bubbling with glee. "You'll make a fine wizard. Your instruction will begin tomorrow. In the morning begin reading the White Book of Magic and I will teach you how to forge your sword and staff." He smiled." What's a wizard without his sword and staff? Your training as a blacksmith will serve you well as it has me when I was your age." Ferryman then addressed the crowd.

"Hail to Beldre! My new apprentice," shouted Ferryman.

"Hail to Beldre! The wizard's apprentice!" shouted the crowd.

Out of the corner of his eye, Ferryman saw Princess Errisa waiting for Beldre. Ferryman placed his hand on Beldre's shoulder, "This is your time. Go and enjoy yourself. I see that a fair maiden is waiting for you?"

Beldre blushed, then went to Errisa and they embraced each other.

"The great wizard Beldre," she said as she leaned forward for a kiss. But the crowd swept Beldre up onto their shoulders and carried him around for all to see, shouting and singing, "Hail to Beldre! The wizard's apprentice!"

Overjoyed, the minstrels played, and everyone sang, danced, and drank.

King Marcus spoke to Ferryman, "What a glorious night and a grand time for you to show off your wizardry and magic."

Ferryman laughed, "Yes, it's time for fireworks!"

Ferryman held aloft the staff of Rume and with a thunderous voice spoke aloud the magic words," Spectardatus Illuminatros!"

A ball of light shot out of the end of his staff and soared high into the sky like a comet, then burst into a brilliant rainbow of colors in the shape of a soaring eagle. Everyone stopped what they were doing and looked to the sky with mesmerized eyes.

"Oh! Ah!" the crowd murmured.

Beldre was free and ran to Errisa who was waiting for him at the center of the grounds. They embraced with a soft-spoken kiss as the fireworks brilliantly transformed the night sky into a dazzlingly delightful, illuminated spectacle.

The End

About the Author

Randy Corn was born September 16, 1960, in Homestead, Florida, the year of Hurricane Donna. Randy had a wonderful childhood as he grew up in Silver Lake, Ohio, and returned to Florida in 1971. Randy started working for GTE/Verizon/Frontier Communications in 1998 and retired after 19 years of service as a telephony drafter/database technician. Randy's passion for storytelling, photography, and cinematography grew into his passion for filmmaking. Randy enrolled in the New York Institute of Photography and graduated on January 14, 2009, with a sense of accomplishment and more enthusiasm to keep learning. After retiring from Frontier Communications in 2016 Randy decided to delve into film photography so Randy embarked on an associate in science degree in Photographic Technology from Saint Petersburg College from which Randy graduated in January 2020. Randy earned his B.A.S. in Technology Management in 2008 and an M.F.A. in Motion Pictures and Television (Screenwriting) in 2014.

Other works available:

The End of Time

Randall Photoshoot Gallery